Melissa Dabrowski, born in Darwen, Lancashire, lives with her son Oscar, husband Tom and three dogs: Rex, Rosie and Luna. Melissa is a full-time funeral director and has a past career in horse racing as a stable hand and amateur jockey. Melissa is a great lover of animals and still rides horses as a hobby. She also owns two thoroughbreds: Anna and Lady. She loves writing and is a keen lover of poetry, relating her work to everyday life experiences that the reader can also relate to.

Melissa Dabrowski

Beyond the Silence

Austin Macauley Publishers
LONDON · CAMBRIDGE · NEW YORK · SHARJAH

Copyright © Melissa Dabrowski 2025

The right of **Melissa Dabrowski** to be identified as author of this work has been asserted by the author in accordance with sections 77 and 78 of the Copyright, Designs and Patents Act 1988.

All rights reserved. No part of this publication may be reproduced, stored in a retrieval system, or transmitted in any form or by any means, electronic, mechanical, photocopying, recording, or otherwise, without the prior permission of the publishers.

Any person who commits any unauthorised act in relation to this publication may be liable to criminal prosecution and civil claims for damages.

A CIP catalogue record for this title is available from the British Library.

ISBN 9781037103933 (Paperback)

ISBN 9781037103940 (ePub e-book)

www.austinmacauley.com

First Published 2025

Austin Macauley Publishers Ltd®

1 Canada Square

Canary Wharf

London

E14 5AA

Special thanks go to some of my close friends, especially to Matt and Albert, who have supported me through this from the very beginning.

It was a new term in September. The sun shone through the clouds in the sky above. Everyone was so excited to start school and to talk about what they had done in the summer holidays, all except for one little girl, Luna, aged nine. A small, shy, quiet girl with brown, straight hair, just touching her shoulders. Luna sat quietly looking out of the school window. All summer, she had watched the world around her carry on as if she didn't exist. She watched young children running around, smiling, playing, and having fun in the park across the street from her house. Luna hated going outside. She had hardly anyone to talk to, and the ones who did try couldn't understand her. This was because Luna was deaf. Nobody at her school knew sign language except her sign language interpreter and helper in her classes. Luna's parents had felt it best for her to go to a mainstream school as opposed to a deaf school. Some of the children in the school laughed at her, called her names, and others would simply avoid her. Luna felt very isolated and depressed.

It was the first day of the new term, and it was going to be the same as it was every year, isolating, depressing, and quiet. Suddenly, the classroom door opened and a new girl walked into the class. Luna sat at the back of the class watching the new girl get introduced. This new girl had long blonde hair, slightly wavy, which flowed past her shoulders to just above the elbow. She held her head high in confidence, not worried about being the new girl in class.

The girl was then shown to her desk by the teacher, which was right next to Luna's.

Luna and the new girl looked at each other. The new girl smiled and started talking. Luna looked at her with sad eyes, trying to lip-read what the new girl was saying to her. Luna pointed to her ears and shook her head, signing that she was deaf. The new girl stopped and looked at Luna. She bent down to her designer bag and pulled out a pink notebook. She opened a page and with her sparkly pink pen, with the fluff on top, she wrote something.

She turned the book to Luna. Luna looked in the book and there was written:

'I'm Emily. What's your name?'

Luna looked up at Emily, beaming at her, for this was the first person in her school to try to have a conversation with her. Emily offered her pen to Luna, prompting her to reply to her message. Luna, without haste, took the pen along with the notebook and wrote back:

'I'm Luna.'

Emily took back the notebook and read it, smiling. She then took the pen and wrote a second time. Luna looked at her wide-eyed, eager to know what she was writing. Emily passed the book back to Luna. Luna looked at what she had written.

'Meet me outside for lunch?'

Luna looked at her and nodded, smiling from ear to ear. They both faced forward towards the teacher, ready for the class to begin.

The bell rang, signalling the start of lunch. All the children packed up their books and pens and headed out the door. Luna followed suit, eager to go and meet Emily. She headed outside to a bench just outside the doors of the school. A few minutes passed, which felt like an eternity for Luna, but through the doors, Emily walked out. Her hair was flowing gently in the autumn breeze. Her designer pink backpack was sitting loosely off one shoulder.

Emily waved over at Luna, who responded with a wave also. Emily joined Luna on the bench and both sat for about a minute, unsure of what to say or do.

Emily pulled her pink notebook back out, along with her pink fluffy pen and started to write. Luna tilted her head a little, trying to look into the notebook so she could get a glimpse of what Emily was writing. Emily turned the book to her and there read the words:

'Can you teach me some basic words, so I can communicate with you?'

Luna nodded at her, excited that someone wanted to try and talk to her, especially in sign, maybe just maybe even be a friend to her. She quickly put her hand to her lips as if she were giving a kiss.

'Thank you,' she mouthed.

Emily responded by copying her, saying the words 'thank you'. Luna clapped her hands in excitement. Luna went on to teach Emily other signs, like good morning, how are you? and friend.

The bell rang again, signalling the end of lunch. Emily pointed at her watch and pointed to the school. Luna already knew the bell had gone, since she felt the vibrations, but thought she'd keep that to herself. Luna followed Emily back to class.

Over the next few weeks, the two girls met up at lunch in the same place and learnt a bit of signing together, building their friendship. By the end of the term, Emily was able to have short conversations with Luna, and she could sign the alphabet.

Unknown to the girls, the teachers had been watching them from the staff room, which was ideally situated across from where the girls would sit and meet up each lunch time. The teachers had often had discussions about Luna's mental health, since this reflected on her schoolwork. She had been failing her lessons due to feeling depressed and isolated. But since Emily had come along, Luna's schoolwork had excelled in every subject! Over the summer holidays, the teachers had plenty of meetings, and one of the topics brought up was about Luna. They discussed how they could help her feel more connected with her peers, which would hopefully help with her school work, with one of the teachers asking, 'Why don't we get someone to teach the children and ourselves basic sign language?' Some teachers were for it while others were against it. They put the question to the Head teacher. He read the reports on Luna and how it had benefited her having someone to talk to. He sat and thought for a moment.

How many people actually know basic sign language? he thought.

He decided to trial a programme which would enable a sign language teacher to come in twice a week to teach the children and the staff basic sign language for six weeks, and at the end of the six weeks, they would be asked if they would like to try out their new skills on an unexpected Luna. To make sure Luna wasn't present when the sign language teacher came in, the Head teacher had arranged for Luna to do one-on-one learning in another classroom with her sign language helper and another member of staff. Luna was a little disappointed she was being removed from class, but she just did as she was told.

Six weeks went by, and Luna was ready to head out for her one-to-one session, but was surprised when she was told to stay in. The class started as normal. She looked at the teacher and noticed that as she was talking, her hands were moving with certain words. Luna sat up straight and watched her teacher in awe! She was signing! Not every word, just some basics, like 'today', 'learning', 'friendship'.

The teacher then asked one of the children, Oscar, to stand up. He stood up and walked to the front of the class. He turned to face the class and pointed at himself, then he pointed at Luna before he signed 'friend'. Luna sat back in her seat, her eyes starting to well up a little. Next minute, a girl two rows in front of Luna stood up. She turned *around to face Luna and signed:*

'Hello. I'm Ebony.'

Luna looked at her in awe! Next minute, half the class stood up. Luna didn't know where to look! Each person took turns to sign a short sentence to Luna.

The last person stood up and walked towards Luna. It was Emily. She smiled at her and took a deep breath. Emily started to sign:

'These few weeks I've known you have been the best I have ever had! You're not just my friend, you're my best friend, thank you for being you!'

Luna jumped up out of her chair and ran over to her, giving her the biggest, tightest hug she could! She stood back and mouthed 'thank you', tears rolling down her face. The two girls embraced again, both hugging each other as tightly as they could.

The Head teacher decided to keep the sign language tutor coming in two days a week, to keep the children updated and learn new signs. He felt the programme may help them for future occurrences with a deaf person, such as Luna. Emily told Luna all that had happened in the last six weeks. Luna couldn't believe it! Why would everyone want to do that for her? Emily explained. *'Nobody hated you; they just felt they couldn't communicate with you. Have a little confidence, and people will try to talk to you. You've always had friends. You just needed a little help to find them.'* Luna responded to Emily, *'How much sign language have you learnt?'* Emily sat back on the bench and laughed to herself. She started to sign. *'I've always known sign language.'* Luna looked at her, puzzled. Emily carried on, *'I'm partially deaf, but my mum is deaf, so the language was taught to me from birth.'*

'Why didn't you tell me?' signed Luna.

'I felt you needed a friend rather than someone who knew sign language,' she said. *'You found it nice that I wanted to learn it, and it made you happy. It gave you a purpose.'*

Luna smiled to herself, looking back on all the times she'd taught Emily something and had never picked up on how quickly Emily had learnt the signs. Emily continued to explain, *'that to overcome her deafness with people, she had to gain confidence. So by walking into the room and standing tall, it's as if she wasn't scared to be there.'*

The two girls became the best of friends, often having other children come up to them asking them to teach them some more signs. Luna felt more connected with the school and even gained new friends, including some who didn't know any signs. The two girls never lost contact with each other. Even after they had both left school and grown up, they were still friends for life, and nothing was to change that.

The End